S0-BAZ-352

ALiEN CLoNES FROM OuTer SPace

Food Fight!

ALIEN CLONES FROM OUTER SPACE

Food Fight!

H. B. Homzie

Matt Phillips

ALADDIN PAPERBACKS

New York   London   Toronto   Sydney   Singapore

H. B. H.: To Grandma Reta
M. P.: To all of us who play with our food

If you purchased this book without a cover, you should be aware that this book is stolen property. It was reported as "unsold and destroyed" to the publisher, and neither the author nor the publisher has received any payment for this "stripped book."

This book is a work of fiction. Any references to historical events, real people, or real locales are used fictitiously. Other names, characters, places, and incidents are the product of the author's imagination, and any resemblance to actual events or locales or persons, living or dead, is entirely coincidental.

First Aladdin Paperbacks edition August 2003

Text copyright © 2003 by H. B. Homzie
Illustrations copyright © 2003 by Matt Phillips

ALADDIN PAPERBACKS
An imprint of Simon & Schuster
Children's Publishing Division
1230 Avenue of the Americas
New York, NY 10020

All rights reserved, including the right of reproduction in whole or in part in any form.

Designed by Sammy Yuen Jr.
The text of this book was set in CentITC Bk BT 13 pt.

Printed in the United States of America
2 4 6 8 10 9 7 5 3 1

Library of Congress Control Number 2002106061
ISBN 0-689-82345-2

Introduction

My name is Barton Jamison and I DO NOT LOVE SCHOOL CAFETERIA FOOD! I repeat: I DO NOT LOVE SCHOOL CAFETERIA FOOD. Sure you might have seen me in the lunchroom yesterday gulping down ring things in fluorescent orange sauce, stuffing Tater Tots in my nose, and inhaling my fruit cup.

But that wasn't me.

It was my clone, Beta. This kid from outer space who looks exactly like me. My twin sister, Nancy, has a clone too. Her name is Gamma.

The clones are on a secret mission to learn about Earth life, so they want to do everything: scrub pots, write book reports, and dissect the DVD player. Of course, Beta and Gamma are new

to Earth ways. So while they have been helping us out, they've also been getting us into major trouble. Last week they shrank a pro basketball player.

It all started in the slime-o-teria. . . .

BARTON:
Out to Lunch

I couldn't eat my ring things or the vegetable medley on my plastic green plate.

I was too nervous.

Skye Johnston was in my school.

My school.

Do you understand how important this is? Do you? Because it's huge. Skye Johnston is the best player in the pros, and the tallest, and the healthiest. He eats only food cooked in peanut oil. And he puts no meat into his body. Not even Slim Jims.

All the other guys at the table were squashing up their food and making mashed Tater Tots.

But not me. Today was the most important day of my life. Except the day the clones landed. That was a pretty big deal too.

As my buddy Ross flattened his chocolate milk

carton with his fist I saw something amazing.

Someone really, really tall passed in front of the cafeteria entrance.

And all I saw was a neck. "That's him!" I screamed. "Look! Look!"

But by the time everyone turned around, he was gone.

"That was Skye Johnston," I insisted, turning to my sister, Nancy. "THE SKYE JOHNSTON. He was wearing a gray shirt. Gray's my favorite color. Hey, I know—let's go after him!"

"Are you crazy, Barton?" said Nancy. "We can't leave the cafeteria without a pass." She pointed to Mrs. Denzer, the cafeteria monitor. We all call her Sarge. Hair is sprouting on her chin, and she blows her whistle every second. She wears the same dress all the time. Rumors are it's an old army uniform.

Slam-dunking his lunch into the trash, a kid yelled, "I'm Skye Johnston!" Sarge blew her whistle.

I pulled my Skye Johnston basketball card out of my backpack. "We've got to go after him. It's our only chance to get an autograph. Probably in our lifetime." I stared at the card. Except for the

2

ketchup stain, it was in great shape.

Skye was smiling in the photo. Of course, I'd be smiling too if I were seven feet tall, that good at jump shots, rich, and liked vegetables.

After lunch Skye was getting the key to our school. In the cafeteria. Well, it's not just a cafeteria. It's kind of a multipurpose room. There's a stage at one end of the room. For Skye's visit they had even set up a basketball net.

Shaking my head, I looked at my sister. "Principal Dumpsy said there'd be no time for autographs. Can you believe it?"

Nancy and I have watched every Skye Johnston game on television. I have two posters of him in my room. Nancy plays basketball for the Pine Bluff Wizards, and she wears Skye's number on her jersey. She even stopped eating meat for a week to be like Skye. We are his biggest fans. We had to get his autograph.

Suddenly an idea popped into my head. "Let's get bathroom passes, and we'll track down Skye."

I didn't have to convince Nancy. Her hand shot up. "Sarge . . . um, I mean, Mrs. Denzer," she called out. "I need a bathroom pass."

"Me too," I said.

Another voice chimed in from the next table. "I need a bathroom pass, Grandma!" It was Otto Denzer, my arch enemy. And Sarge just happened to be his grandma. Otto pointed to a kid sitting at the other end of his table who was quietly eating his lunch. "And so does Archie."

Sarge hiked down the aisle toward our table. Her linebacker body rocked and her double chins flapped together as if they were clapping. Then she smiled at Nancy and me.

We were getting those passes. I could feel it! In the two hundred years Sarge has worked in the lunchroom at Pine Bluff Elementary School, she has never smiled at anyone before.

"Otto and Archie get the passes," Sarge barked, pointing at Nancy and me. "You're next."

Racing past me toward the door, Otto kicked my chair. Other kids looked up as he ran by.

"Next?" I said, panicking. We didn't have time to wait. Skye Johnston wouldn't be in the hallway of Pine Bluff Elementary School forever.

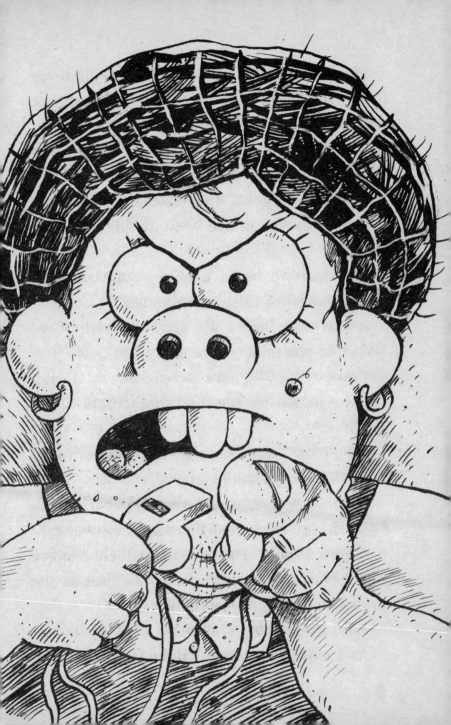

"What do we do?" I sputtered, looking helplessly at Nancy. With her back to us, Sarge waddled away. Nancy grabbed my hand. "Let's make a break for it." We zoomed toward the door. Sneaking into the hallway, we ducked behind the lockers. The exact same hallway that Skye Johnston had been in only moments before!

Suddenly we heard a noise. Somebody big slouched against the water fountain.

It was Otto Denzer. He glared at both of us. "What do you think you're doing?"

"We . . . uh . . . have stomachaches," I said. "We're going to the bathroom. You know, *the food.*"

"The food?" asked Otto, stepping closer to my face. "Whaddaya talking about?"

"The steak fingers are real fingers," I said. "Why do you think the cafeteria ladies wear rubber gloves, huh? They're hiding their stumps. And they call the pork 'dinosaur bits' because the meat's so old." I laughed weakly.

But I guess Otto didn't think it was so funny.

As I looked down the hallway for Skye, Otto

waved a fist in front of my nose. "That's my grandma's cafeteria you're talking about."

"Grandma!" he shouted. "Guess who's in the hallway! Without a bathroom pass!" Then he sneered at us. "Your life is over."

Storming through the swinging door, he disappeared into the cafeteria.

Nancy stared at the freshly waxed linoleum floor. "We're in big trouble," she said.

My heart sank into my feet. But then I got an idea. "Quick. Call the clones," I said. "We'll switch places with them and get Skye's autograph."

"I don't know if calling the clones is such a good idea," Nancy said.

"It's our only hope," I pleaded. "Anyway, I bet today's special is good for aliens. What could go wrong?"

My sister folded her arms across her chest. "Last time we let the clones baby-sit for us, they turned the kid into an alien dog—a *woozie*. Remember?"

"It'll be different this time," I promised, unzipping the outside pocket of my fanny pack. That's where I keep the *snogelplat*, otherwise known as the clone phone. You push a button, and Beta and Gamma can beam themselves to wherever you are.

I whipped out the clone phone and pressed the purple button. A millisecond later bright lights flashed and sparkled around us. Beta appeared in the water fountain.

"Greetings!" he said. He was dressed in my clothes—a pair of jeans and a red turtleneck. Except for the goofy grin, Beta was my exact double.

"Where are we?" asked Beta.

Nancy nodded at the row of lockers. "You're at Pine Bluff Elementary School. Outside the lunchroom."

As Beta rubbed his hands together, Gamma appeared, hanging from the blinking fluorescent lights. Except for her retractable antennae, she looked exactly like my sister.

Gamma threw out her arms. "I'm slipping and heading for a crash landing. Prepare for deep impact!" She dropped down to the floor and sniffed the air. "AH! THE LUNCHROOM! No wonder it smells so wonderful. My two stomachs are growling in anticipation."

Nancy gave me a told-you-so look.

"I want to wait in line," said Beta, jumping out of the water fountain. "My sister and I have seen Earth videos, as a part of our training, where kids stand around for hours for the honor of eating school cafeteria food."

Gamma pointed her antennae toward the lunchroom door. "I want to eat canned food in fluorescent orange sauce, and I understand the trays are edible, too. That would be so messy. I mean, neat!"

"Listen guys, calm down," Nancy said. "Just zip in, without anyone seeing you, into the cafeteria. That's where we're supposed to be. Sit and smile and do nothing."

"Otto's trying to get us in trouble," I explained. "He's getting his grandma. His . . . her name is Sarge, and she's the cafeteria monitor."

"I WANT TRIPLE SERVINGS!" yelled Beta, patting his stomach. "TRIPLE YUM!"

I smiled at Beta and Gamma. "All you have to do is pretend you're us. We're getting autographs from Skye Johnston. We'll be back before the bell rings."

Beta rubbed his elbows together. "Thank you for thinking of us. We cannot wait to consume cafeteria food. It is a supreme honor!"

Chapter 2

BeTA:
Ring Thing Fling

Using our rocket-powered boots, Gamma and I zipped into the cafeteria undetected. We sat down with our Earth clones' friends. Many blew on straws filled with little green balls, known as peas. Some of the humans beat on the table in some sort of primitive battle chant.

As we sat down to eat, the overgrown earthling known as Otto whizzed by us. "Grandma!" he shouted. "Nancy and Barton are in the hallway. See?"

"No, they're not," said the earthling known as Sarge.

Otto stared at Gamma and me sitting at the table. His head wagged back and froth. "But . . . but . . . but they were just in the hallway a second ago," he blabbered.

Sarge, the great leader of the cafeteria, smiled

at Otto. "Let Grandma go back and get you some extra-special crispy turkey nuggets. Okay, pumpkin?" Some of the earthlings chortled with happiness.

Otto nodded and then sprang over to us. "I don't know how you guys got back here so fast." He stared at our plates. "You're eating that up!"

"You really wish us to consume these food products?" I inquired.

"Yup!" shouted Otto. "There better not be a single ring thing left on your plate!" He danced in a circle around the table, singing, "Ring-a-rama, yeah! Ring-a-licious, yeah!"

Gamma happily scooped up something brown, and I excitedly scooped up orange mush, which wiggled back and forth on my fork. It looked like *gingok* larvae. Back on Ungapotch it is my favorite meal.

A giant glob from my fork spattered all over Otto's shoes. Little chunks covered the bottom of his pants. A string of goop dangled from the end of his nose. He was so lucky! I love to lick *gingko* off my nose.

Otto grabbed a napkin and wiped his face.

"You're going to eat crow!" he screamed.

"Crow? Yum!" I opened my mouth extra wise and waited for the bird. Otto took a plate of food and smashed it into my face.

"*Zaptopkaka!* Thank you, overgrown one," I said, licking the food substance, which was dribbling off my chin.

Then I stuffed the material as fast as I could into my mouth and nose. But I was being so rude. I hadn't asked the overgrown one if he wanted any food.

Since the invention called the fork took too much time, I smashed the plate of larvae into his face. I shouted, "Consume, my friend!" Students turned from their tables to watch, nudging one another and laughing.

Otto must have really liked me, because he picked up a substance known as green Jell-O and pounded it into my hair. My follicles were certainly being well nourished. Then Gamma took a carton of chocolate cow milk and dumped it all over Otto's head.

"FOOD FIGHT!" screamed the earthlings. Fight? It was a feast. We were feeding each other.

I would have to make note of this in my *totopa-pap* journal.

Others were soon feasting as well, dumping platters of meatballs into one another's hair and slinging orange mush.

Otto grabbed cow milk and dumped it on Gamma's head. This was so much fun! Barton and Nancy were so kind to let us participate in this lunchroom feast.

For a moment I felt a tear roll down my cheek. I was actually homesick for a second, thinking about dear old Ungapotch and my favorite restaurant, the Goopgunk Pod.

I slurped up the rest of my meal. Then, using the reverse vacuum power of my spare stomach, I sprayed the food across the room. It flew past Otto, sliming his shirt and the wall behind him.

Using her pinkie finger, Gamma threw ring things, and they landed perfectly on a cafeteria worker's ear unit. What lovely jewelry they made. The earthling seemed very excited about her new look. As the ring rolled down her face unit, she screamed, "Monitor! Monitor!"

Sarge stormed into the center of the lunchroom. She blew the whistle, which made a sweet sound like that of an Ungapotchian snorthog.

The feeding continued.

Mashed potatoes landed on Sarge's head unit. I blew some delicious gravy over her way. The cafeteria leader would be so pleased.

As gravy dripped off Sarge's nose unit she blew the whistle again. "Stop! I've had enough!" How strange. The cafeteria leader had hardly eaten a thing.

Otto pointed at my sister and me. "Barton and Nancy Jamison started everything."

"Everything," echoed the cafeteria worker from the lunch line as she picked ring things out of her ears.

I smiled. "Yes, I did it. I take full responsibility!"

"I participated as well," added Gamma. "In fact, I threw many more vegetables, which are highly nutritious." Many of the earthlings laughed with happiness.

I felt proud that Otto had noticed our skill at feeding.

Sarge, the great cafeteria leader, whipped out a pink slip. "See this? You know what this is?"

We shook our heads. "I've never seen such a piece of fiber like that. It is a most attractive color, like that of the Zeezak moon," I said. Some of the students looked puzzled. I forgot that earthlings don't know their astronomy very well.

"It's a suspension slip!" screamed Sarge.

"Suspension?" I asked. "From where? Upside down and from a tree?"

I watched Barton's friends exchange glances at one another, shrugging. What a strange thing to do.

Sarge waved a clipboard. "I'm calling the principal!" She pointed at the cafeteria walls, decorated with food.

"We were supposed to have a very important assembly here," screamed Sarge, "with Skye Johnston." She blew her whistle. "You will be made examples of."

Gamma smiled. My blood-pumping machine beat rapidly. Made an example of? Famous? All of the eyes in the cafeteria were upon us. We were being given a medal called a pink slip!

The great cafeteria leader handed Gamma and me the delicate pink paper. Shakily I took the slip

PINK SLIP

Barton and
Nancy Jamison
to the
Principal's Office!

from her fingers and pinned it onto my shirt. Then I wiped larvae all over it. We were now decorated heroes.

Nancy and Barton would be so proud. They would have the opportunity to visit the great leader, the principal. And we had earned them the pink slip!

Chapter 3

BARTON:
He's All That

Nancy and I rushed down the hallway. Skye Johnston had to be nearby. He wasn't someone who could easily hide in something like a locker or stuff himself into a gym bag.

"Where do you think he could be?" asked Nancy.

"Try the teachers' lounge," I suggested.

She pointed to the sign that said FACULTY ONLY. "We can't go there. That's where teachers drink coffee and watch soaps."

"Just keep quiet and act like we're supposed to be there," I said, opening the door.

And guess what?

He was there. Alone.

Skye Johnston. *The* Skye Johnston.

It was one thing to see his neck pass by the cafeteria. And another thing to see the whole of him up close.

19

First of all, he was really big. I mean it. His feet were longer than ten rolls of toilet paper.

He wore glasses. And was reading a book.

"Hi, Skye!" I shouted, forgetting about being quiet. I whipped out my basketball card. "Skye, could you sign this. Please? Please?"

"And my shirt?" asked Nancy, turning around.

When Skye stood up, I thought his head was going to hit the ceiling. "I'd be happy to sign some autographs," he said, smiling.

Nancy pulled a camera out of her backpack. "I wish I could take a picture of all three of us together."

Skye shrugged. "Hey, I'd ask the principal, but he just got called out to some emergency in the cafeteria."

"Did you just say the cafeteria?" I asked.

"Yes, I did," said Skye, nodding.

I started to panic. That's where we'd left the clones.

"We better go," said Nancy, smiling nervously. "And see if everybody is okay."

I couldn't believe this was happening. I felt so disappointed. As Nancy and I flew out the door

Skye shouted, "What about your autographs?"

"Another time," I replied, thinking there'd probably never be another time.

"Skye, you're the greatest," Nancy hollered back. "We'll never forget you!"

And I'll never forget that moment. It was so unfair. We were just about to get those autographs. "What do you think the clones did?" I asked, huffing down the hall.

"I don't want to think about it," said Nancy.

We stood in front of the cafeteria door. I went to push it open, when Nancy pulled my shirt. "Whoa," she said. "The clones are still in there. Let's just peek in and see what's up."

I stood on my tiptoes and looked in through the little window at the top of the door.

"What's going on?" asked Nancy.

I groaned. "It's not good."

Ketchup dotted the ceiling, mashed potatoes coated the backs of the chairs, gravy dripped down off the light fixtures. Half the kids were trying to wipe themselves off with napkins. But the orange mush was eating right through the paper.

Principal Dumpsy and Sarge paced the room, handing out pink slips. Beta and Gamma already had their pink slips pinned onto their chests.

The place was a huge mess, and I had this feeling the clones were in the middle of it!

Chapter 4

BeTA:

Shrink in a Wink

The light flashed on the *snogelplat*. It was my Earth clone, Barton. He wanted us to clean up the cafeteria zone and slurp everyone's brain cells. Especially Principal Dumpsy's and Sarge's.

"*Hoopla. Hoopla!*" said Gamma. "We get some more brain Slurpees."

I took my time wrinkler out of my activity belt.

"What are you doing?" screamed Sarge, staring at my time wrinkler. "No toys in the cafeteria. And I said, heads down on the desk. Do you understand English?"

"Not entirely," I replied, taking time out of the wrinkler, which looks like what earthlings call blue Play-Doh. I squished it in my hand.

"STOP!" screamed Sarge, pointing at me with her clipboard.

The boy called Otto stood up, waving his

arms. "What are you doing?" he asked. "Hey, what's that? Hey, wait a minute. I'm remembering something. From last week. You . . . you . . . you're not Barton."

"Correct, Earthling," I said. "My name is Beta Zeeekwarplatzatot."

"You're not from this planet," he babbled.

That's when I activated the time wrinkler. The whole room spun around like an Earth merry-go-round. The room started to fold and crease like a giant wrinkle.

"Wrinkle activated," I said. "Time will be frozen for 2.5 *gigazaps*."

Otto froze and floated up to the ceiling, as did the rest of the earthlings. They looked like very festive party balloons.

I took the brain straws out. It was time to suck up select memory cells! As I slurped out Principal Dumpsy's brain cells, then the cafeteria workers' and all the kids', Gamma licked all the food decorations off the walls.

When I got to Sarge, I had trouble finding her brain. "It must be in here somewhere," I said. I kept on poking.

"Don't worry about Sarge," said Gamma as she licked the peas off the ceiling in hyperwarp speed. "Her brain probably isn't fully functional anyway."

Gamma whirled around, staring at the cafeteria. "This feeding facility appears so ordinary," she said. "I think it needs to be fixed up."

Together we attached a small meteorite and some alien flashing lights to the ceiling. The chairs were adjusted to account for the height of each student and for the curvature of the earth.

With the napkins, I created little space pods. Gamma then proceeded to make orange mush roses and swans out of ring things.

As I hung some mashed potatoes from the ceiling to look like clouds, a small, furry rodent ran under my feet.

"*Zaptopkaka*, it's a mouse," I announced.

In hyperwarp speed Gamma trapped it in her hands. "Let us shrink it and take it back as a specimen to Commander Zortek," said Gamma. "He will be most pleased. We can use the *blip-sprock*."

Gamma sprayed green liquid out of a tiny metal canister onto a plate.

I jumped up and down. "Yes, stellar idea, Sister. Use *blip-sprock* and feed it to the mouse."

Gamma set down the plate full of *blip-sprock*. The mouse creature took two licks and was shrunk to the size of a *minatutu*, the smallest creature on our planet.

I took a plastic test tube out of my fanny pack and flicked the mini mouse, which was now the size of an Earth flea, inside.

"What else can we do, Sister, to help?" That's when I noticed a paper posted with the menu for the next day. "It says 'tossed salad.' Let us toss." I took a giant head of lettuce and threw it to my sister. "This is an enjoyable activity."

The next item on the menu was a food product called egg rolls. I reached into the refrigeration unit and pulled out five dozen eggs. "Time for egg rolls!" I shouted.

Gamma rolled her eggs down one side of the kitchen while I rolled my eggs down the other side.

Suddenly a giant earthling zoomed into the kitchen. He nodded at us and put his fingers to his lips.

"We're rolling eggs," I said.

"Stop it, they'll hear," the giraffelike earthling whispered. "Reporters. They're after me," he said, tapping his chest. "Skye Johnston." He crouched next to the refrigeration unit.

"Would you like an egg roll?" asked Gamma.

She bowled a dozen eggs. They rolled and cracked against his feet. Egg yolk covered the floor. It was the color of the Morkoko asteroid belt.

Skye jumped back. "What are you doing?" He looked around, grabbed a towel, and brushed off his shoes. "You guys have got to calm down." Then he blinked a few times. "Hey, aren't you the kids from the teachers' lounge?"

I shook my head. "Negative. We are not from the teachers' lounge. We are from the Zorillion Galaxy."

Laughing, Skye shook his head. "Okay, whatever you say. Ever thought about a career in show business?" Suddenly he stared at the *blipsprock* on the plate. "Hey, what's that?" He patted his stomach unit. "Is that vegetarian?"

"Ungapotchian," stated Gamma proudly.

Skye stepped toward the plate of shrinking goo. "Wow. You mean that restaurant in L.A.? I love that place. They don't serve meat in that place. There's no meat in this, right?"

I nodded. *Blip-sprock*, renowned shrinking formula, is composed of the slime that lives in the sewage system on Ungapotch. "There is no meat," I stated. "You are correct."

The tall one sniffed. "Smells good. I'm starved." He started to reach for the food.

"That is not a good idea," said Gamma. Her eyes grew as big as the flying saucers that crowd the intergalactic freeway.

Chapter 5

BeTA:
Lay Low

Suddenly, Skye jumped back behind the refrigeration unit. "Shhh," he said. "They're coming back. The reporters. Sometimes I wish I could be two inches tall."

An earthling popped in through the doorway. He wore a camera around his neck. "Is Skye Johnston here?" He looked around at the egg yolk and heads of lettuce all over the floor. Then he looked at my sister and me and raced down the hall.

The tall earthling sighed and came up from behind the frozen food. "I need to lay low for a while. Almost be invisible."

"Lay low?" asked Gamma. "Almost invisible?"

I looked at my sister. And she looked at me. "We must give this earthling his wish," I said.

Gamma picked up a big plate of *blip-sprock*

and presented it to Skye. "Here, please consume this. It will shrink you and make you feel extremely small."

Skye rubbed his hands together. "A new type of energy food. Excellent." He grabbed a fork and consumed the *blip-sprock*. "Mmm, this is great! What did you put in it? It's out of this world."

His eyes swirled around like a comet. Little stars floated around his head.

Then his head shrank to the size of a walnut. "Man, I feel good," said Skye in a high, squeaky voice. "Like I've taken a load off."

Gamma and I happily clapped our hands. We were helping this earthling so much. He could now lay low.

Next Skye's body began to shrivel like a raisin.

His left foot became the size of a peanut. And so did his right foot. Except for his big toe. It burst out of his shoe. The toenail first.

Skye spun around and stared at the kitchen. "Hey, what's happening to me? The room . . . it's huge. And you . . ." He pointed to Gamma and me. "You're giants! Are you basketball players? The fridge is gigantic too. Everything's really,

really huge, or else I am really, really small."

"You are extremely small," I explained. "Two inches, to be exact."

"We shrank you," Gamma responded with much glee. "And now we must shrink your left toe, too," said Gamma. She held up the rest of the plate of the *blip-sprock*. "Here!"

Skye raced away from us. "He's playing a game," I said. "This is extremely fun." As Gamma reached down to feed him more *blip-sprock*, Skye ducked under the sink.

The little man wouldn't stay still.

"Ow!" he yelled. "What's the giant hunk of moldy cheese? That's sick!" He plugged up his nose. "Peyew!" A metal trap slammed down on his leg. "A mousetrap! Ow!" he screamed.

As Gamma freed Skye, I smeared his toe with *blip-sprock*.

The toenail shrank. And then his toe did, too.

Gamma noted the time machine mounted on the wall. "We must deactivate the time wrinkler!" I grabbed Skye and stuffed him into my pant pocket.

"Put me down," yelled Skye in a little voice. "What are you doing?"

"Placing you in my pocket," I said.

Dashing into the cafeteria, Gamma and I jammed our little fingers together.

"*MUCKA MUCKA* pinkie power!" we shouted, unleashing a new energy field, which unfroze the earthlings floating at the top of the cafeteria. They would wake up in one half a *gigazap*. As we had slurped up their memory cells, they would have no memory of what happened. All except for Sarge, of course.

Hoopla. Hoopla. We had decorated the cafeteria and shrank Skye Johnston. Barton and Nancy would be so pleased.

Chapter 6

BARTON:
It's a Small World

I high-fived Nancy. "You see," I said, peeking out of our hiding spot in the custodian's closet, "I told you using the clones was a good idea. Beta told me they cleaned up the cafeteria and that they did something special for Skye."

Nancy grabbed the clone phone from me. "Okay, that's great." She pushed the purple button. "We're ready to switch places."

A beam of silver light streaked around us, and then suddenly we were back in the cafeteria, sitting in our usual seats.

I looked around me. All the kids were acting really sleepy. Like they were waking up from some kind of nap.

The cafeteria looked like an alien amusement park. There were fluffy clouds and crazy lights. All

35

of the tables were topsy-turvy, and some kind of little planet thing hung from the ceiling.

This was looking alien weird. I suddenly felt like disappearing.

"What happened?" asked Principal Dumpsy, scratching his head. "Why am I holding fifty pink slips?" He narrowed his eyes. "It's coming back to me now."

He studied Sarge. "You said this place was a mess."

"A disaster," insisted Sarge.

Principal Dumpsy looked around the room. "Where? I see a polished floor and no more spit-balls on the ceiling." He ran his hands along the bottoms of the tables. "All the gum's gone! You even had the kids put up decorations. I love the disco ball. Nice touch. And the clouds, too. C'mon, you said the place was a mess for a nice little joke, right? Well, you got me. You certainly did. My heart was pounding. With Skye here, I thought I was going to be a goner." Principal Dumpsy pushed Sarge on the shoulder. "You kidder, you!"

Sarge waved a packet of pink slips into the

air. "I am not a kidder! I don't make jokes. This room . . ."

Then Sarge looked around the room. Her eyes grew big. She blinked. And then she started knocking her head with her fist.

"It was a mess. I don't know . . . how . . . oh, my goodness," Sarge said, covering her face. "It was a food fight. The worst I've ever seen in forty years. Nothing like it. And now . . . oh, my . . . oh, oh . . ."

Kids were looking on, whispering and shaking their heads.

"Maybe you should sit, Grandma," said Otto. "You're sounding a little weird."

Principal Dumpsy shook his head. "Weird is right. This place is cleaner than I've ever seen it."

I couldn't believe it. The clones had done something right for a change. The principal smiled. "Who's responsible for these wonderful decorations?"

Nancy and I stepped forward. "We are, Mr. Dumpsy!"

"Barton and Nancy Jamison," said Mr. Dumpsy, "you deserve some kind of honor." He tapped his chin. "I'll tell you what I'm going to do. I want you to go to the teachers' lounge and personally escort Skye Johnston backstage for the assembly. I need you to get him right now. How does that sound?"

Nancy and I jumped up and down. "Oh, Mr. Dumpsy! Thank you, thank you!"

I shot my hands up in a victory salute. Nancy's friends were jumping up and down, and my buddy Ross gave me a big thumbs-up.

Smiling, Mr. Dumpsy threw his stack of pink slips into the trash. "A million reporters are here, and Skye Johnston is getting the key to our school. It's going to be a great day at Pine Bluff Elementary!" He turned to Nancy and me. "Go to it, kids."

I couldn't believe our good luck. In a few minutes we'd be personally escorting Skye Johnston. And we would finally get our autographs. "Life is sweet!" I yelled.

Nancy and I raced down the hall to the teachers' lounge and opened the door. Beta and Gamma were watching TV. What were the clones doing there?

"Boy, are we having a good time with Skye!" said Beta.

I smiled. "See, I told you, Nance. Everything's

fine. They're keeping Skye company. Wasn't that thoughtful?"

Nancy whirled around. "But where is he? I don't see him anywhere."

"Right here in the room," said Gamma, grinning. Then I heard something. Kind of muffled. A tiny voice. It was so tiny I couldn't make out the words.

"Yes, Skye has not stopped talking," said Beta. "I think he's very excited. Ever since we fed him *blip-sprock*."

"*Blip-sprock?* What's that?" I asked.

"Food with alien shrinking powder," stated Beta.

"SHRINKING POWDER!" screamed Nancy.

That's when a little hand waved from Beta's pocket.

And then a little head popped out. An itsy-bitsy man hopped out, hung on to a button, and dropped onto a small table.

It was Skye Johnston. At least, a mini version of him.

"Is that who I think it is?" I asked, my voice wavering. "Is that Skye?"

He stood no bigger than my little toe. The size of a bite-size Tootsie Roll! A golf ball was three times the size of his head. I couldn't believe my eyes.

Skye screamed, "HELP!" He sounded like he had sucked in ten helium balloons. "I'm tiny!" he yelled in his paper-thin voice. "Help me!"

Nancy looked at me. Her face had turned completely red.

This is not happening, I tried to tell myself.

I pointed to the poster of a tall Skye Johnston in front of us. "Skye Johnston. That's his name 'cause he's tall. His head touches the clouds." I stared at the clones. "How are we going to explain to four hundred kids sitting in an assembly that the world's tallest player is now the world's smallest player?"

"You've got to unshrink Skye! Now!" Nancy screamed.

"Yeah!" squeaked Skye.

Gamma raised her antennae. "Oh, *tinglewarp!*" she muttered. Then she started to smile. "I know! We will make *uta-goola*, a growing formula. It simply requires the hair from an Earth leader. We will obtain this hair, mix the formula, and make him big again."

Immediately Beta and Gamma flew out the door.

"Hurry!" I screamed. "We're running out of time. The assembly starts in five minutes."

A fan sat on the other end of the table. It blew Skye backward. He grabbed hold of a magazine. But his grip wasn't strong enough.

He flew into the air, landing in a Styrofoam cup of coffee. I guess some teacher had left it.

"Help!" Skye screamed, bopping up and down in the black, murky coffee. "I hate coffee!"

BARTON:
An Unusual Prize

Skye helplessly sank into the black murky liquid. "Help!" he screamed.

"Don't worry, Skye!" I yelled. "We'll get you out of there." I quickly pulled a pack of Life Savers out of my pocket and threw him a cherry one. Skye looked like a string bean stranded on a life preserver.

"Here!" I said. "Hang on!" As Skye grabbed hold of the Life Saver, Nancy pulled him out of the cup of coffee.

"I am so sorry, Mr. Johnston," I said. "I know you're really mad, and I know you used to be really big. But I want you to know that I am your biggest fan. I know it's not the best time to ask for your autograph again, but . . ."

Nancy stared at me, shaking her head no.

"Okay, I know maybe it's not the best time

right now," I rushed. "But remember when . . . you get big . . . who made you big . . . again. I know you used to be big, and all . . . here." I placed my basketball card at his feet. And then I handed Skye a pencil.

Skye bear-hugged the pencil. He held on to it with all of his might. His face tightened. "Grrr," he groaned in a voice as deep as a cricket.

"Skye? Do you need help holding that pencil?" asked Nancy.

"No," he snapped. "Skye Johnston can hold a pencil. Sheesh." The pencil started to waver. It tipped backward and it rolled down the desk with Skye still holding on.

It rolled to the edge of the table.

And stopped.

Standing up, Skye waved me over. "C'mere!" he shouted.

I bent down. My nose was next to his little teeny tiny head.

"Closer!" he said. I leaned farther down.

Then he kicked me right in the nose. "Ow!" I yelled.

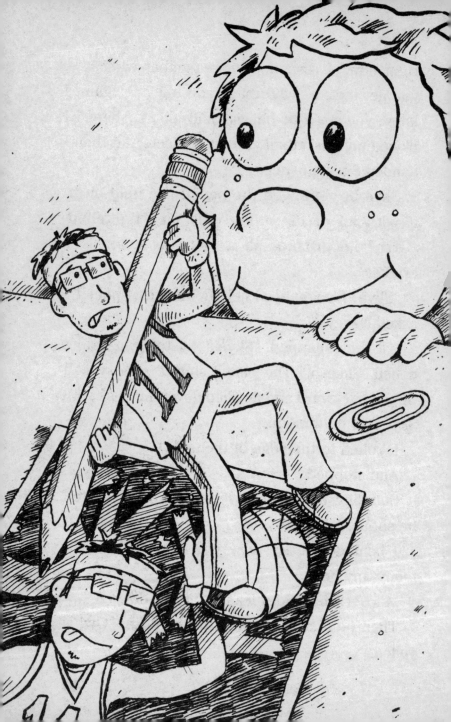

"Get me out of here!" he yelled in his little voice. "Make me big!"

At that moment a fly buzzed by Skye. I guess he was hungry. The fly, that is.

"It's Godzilla! Get that thing away from me." He jumped and grabbed the pencil. "Back!" he screamed.

I swatted the fly with a math book.

"We need to put you some place safe," said Nancy. "Like a little dollhouse. You could get crushed in a pocket." She looked around the room. "Any cotton around for a little bed? Wouldn't that be cute?"

"I am *not* cute," said Skye.

Nancy found a box of Cracker Jack sitting on a table and ripped off the top. "See, I'll make you a little bed," she said, setting the box on the table. "And a house with little curtains."

"You people are crazy!" screamed Skye. Suddenly he slipped on a drop of soda and tumbled into the Cracker Jack.

At that moment Otto burst into the room. "Where's Skye?" he panted. "Principal Dumpsy told me to tell you guys to hurry up."

"Sk-Skye?" I stuttered, glancing at the box of Cracker Jack. "Uh . . . he went to get a drink of water. Down the hall, but don't go after him. He wants to be alone."

Otto's eyes shifted to the little table. He smiled. "I love Cracker Jack." Tilting the box back, he tapped caramel corn into his mouth. *Crunch. Crunch. Crunch.*

He could be snapping off Skye's head, I thought.

"Stop!" I yelled, pointing to the box. "Those are bad for you. You'll get cavities. Please stop!"

Otto popped more Cracker Jack into his mouth.

"That's my box of Cracker Jack," pleaded Nancy.

"Oh, yeah," Otto said, crunching down on the caramel corn.

"No, it's . . . not good," I babbled. "I . . . uh . . . sneezed on it."

"Yeah, right," said Otto, rolling his eyes. He held up the box and opened his mouth extra wide.

At the top of the box I could see Skye's hand. He'd be eaten any second!

Tiny screams suddenly pierced the room.

Otto whipped around. "Who's screaming?"

"Uh . . . me," said Nancy, patting her stomach. "I ate too many ring things. Ow. Ow."

As Nancy talked about her tummy ache Skye screamed again. Only louder. And higher.

Otto looked around the room. "Now who's screaming?"

I hopped up and down on my left foot. "OW! Ew! I stubbed my toe! It hurts! Ow! Major pain!" Lunging forward, I grabbed the box of Cracker Jack.

But Otto wouldn't let go.

As we tugged it back and forth I watched Skye slide back into the box.

"Give it back to me, Bart Fart!" screamed Otto.

"No," I yelled, yanking it away. I threw the box over my head to Nancy. Only I guess I didn't throw it high enough, because Otto grabbed it again.

Skye had clawed his way up. He was hanging off the top, and was about to drop to the floor, when Otto shook the box. Skye slid right back down into the package of caramel corn. He was probably down at the bottom with the prize.

Otto squinted his eyes. "I don't know what's up with you. You act like there's something special about this." He shook the box. "It's just Cracker Jack." He threw the box into his backpack.

Laughing evilly, he dashed out the door.

Chapter 8

BETA:

Chin Up

Using our rocket-powered boots, we zipped into the cafeteria in less than a *hipabyte*. I could hear Mr. Dumpsy, the great leader of the school, talking. "In a few moments I will present to you Skye Johnston!"

The kids burst into applause. "Skye!" they chanted. "Skye! Skye! Skye!"

"We don't have much time, Sister," I observed. "These excited earthlings are expecting the giraffe-like earthling very, very soon. We must hurry."

Gamma nodded. "The time is rotten to get the hair. I mean, the time is ripe," she corrected.

I prepared to walk across the cafeteria chamber, when I noticed something. Mr. Dumpsy was completely bald.

I stared at Gamma. "What do we do now?" I asked.

"In the kitchen," said Gamma. "There sits the great leader of the cafeteria, known as Sarge. I observed plentiful hair on her chin."

In hyperwarp speed, to avoid detection, we flew into the kitchen. I pointed to a woman gobbling a mound of orange mush and ring things. "There is the great leader of the cafeteria!"

Sarge wobbled around. "What are you two doing here? Where's Skye? You're supposed to bring him back to the cafeteria."

"There's been a slight delay," I announced. "But we will rectify it soon. Pull out your chin hair, hand it over, and we'll be on our way."

"A chin hair? I don't have a chin hair. Do I?" She stroked her fingers along her chin. "Oh, my. Oh, my."

"See, they are plentiful!" I shouted.

Sarge wagged her finger at us. "Does your mother know how you behave?"

Gamma shook her head. "Oh, no, Great Leader of the Cafeteria. We were raised by robots."

With our rocket-powered boots, we flipped upside down and hovered over the great leader of the cafeteria. I whipped out the ionized-chamber follicle remover. "Time to remove the chin hair of the earthling."

"No!" yelled Sarge. "What are you doing? How did you kids do that?" She stared as we flew over her head.

Then she grabbed a broom and chased after us.

Gamma hid behind the refrigerator unit while I prepared the ionized-chamber follicle remover.

Sarge scooped up a handful of leftovers and threw them at us.

A miniature hot dog bonked me on the head. I immediately used my antennae to stab the long, tasty treat, and I ate it.

"Take that, you freaky children!" screamed Sarge as she slung sliced peaches at Gamma.

I pointed the ionized-chamber follicle remover at the subject. *"Vramp vrok wit!"*

A tornado force squeezed into one little area— Sarge's chin.

She blew backward, grabbing on to the handle of the microwave oven.

"GOT IT!" I said happily. Then I stared at the hair follicle. "It is not very long. To be safe, we need another one."

"Stay away from me," said Sarge, throwing some brussels sprouts at Gamma. I immediately turned the ionized-chamber follicle remover back on and got a much longer piece of chin hair.

"Ow!" screamed Sarge. "I'm reporting you to the principal!"

Gamma liquidated the chin hair with her pinkie power. Then I blew on it and vaporized the formula. With our *xacro* ray, we let it bake. In less than half a *gigazap* we'd made the antidote.

I touched the hard pink sphere. "It is ready."

"Hoopla!" said Gamma. "We must vacate!"

Launching ourselves in our rocket-powered boots, we exclaimed, "Time to unshrink Skye!"

Chapter 9

BARTON:
Zipped, Sealed, and Delivered

As Otto raced down the hallway Nancy and I jogged behind, desperately trying to catch up.

Cupping her hands, Nancy called out to Skye, "We love you. We're sorry about everything, but we promise we'll make it up to you. Soon."

Otto stopped and whipped around. "Who are you talking to?"

"Nobody?" I shrugged.

"No, I heard you talking, saying that you love me," insisted Otto.

"Because we do," said Nancy. "We think you are so smart and so cool. The most awesome dude ever. You're almost as cool as . . . as . . . Skye Johnston."

Looking at Nancy, Otto tapped his chin. "You think I'm cool?"

Nancy nodded. "Oh, yeah. Really cool. You eat,

burp, slurp down your food. Could I have your autograph?"

"And could I try on your backpack?" I asked.

"Sure," said Otto, grinning.

I slipped the backpack on. "I want to feel as cool as you."

"Barton, you really think I'm cool?" asked Otto.

"I think you're gross," I sputtered without thinking. "I mean, cool," I corrected.

Otto grabbed the backpack away from me. "You can't have it. No-a-rama. No-a-licious!" He stared at me with his beady eyes. "Why do you really want my backpack? I know you're up to something, Bart Fart!"

As Otto's fist waved in front of my nose I took a step backward.

"Uh . . . well," I stammered. "You see . . ."

Otto's eyes crossed and his fist grew closer.

I had no choice but to tell him the truth. Taking a deep breath, I said, "What happened is we have alien clones from outer space, and they shrank Skye, so that he's only two inches high. And they went to find the antidote to make him big again, so they are going to suck out the hair from somebody. And . . ."

Otto's eyes screwed up. His eyes darted back and forth. "You guys are insane. You expect me to believe there's a little two-inch man inside my backpack? No, not just a regular two-inch guy. But Skye Johnston? Get real!"

"Help me!" said a little voice.

"Who said that?" asked Otto, whirling around. "I heard something coming from my backpack."

"Me!" said Skye.

"My backpack!" yelled Otto. "It's talking to me!" Then he whacked his head. "I must be crazy. Backpacks don't talk." He looked at Nancy and me. "You're tricking me. Throwing your voice or something."

Raising his backpack over his head, he said, "I'm putting this some place safe. For a long, long time." He pointed to a tall orange locker next to him. "See that locker? That's my locker. And I'm going to put *my* backpack into *my* locker."

I watched as Otto twirled the combination to his locker.

I couldn't let him do it.

Skye could be trapped inside a Cracker Jack box inside of Otto's smelly backpack inside of a locker forever.

Otto gave his evil laugh. "You can't get it this time, Bart Fart!"

"NO!" I yelled as Otto slammed his locker shut. "NOOOOO!"

Chapter 10

BETA:

You Are What You Eat

"**W**e have created the antidote—the *uta-goola*," I announced to our Earth clones as we landed in the hallway. I could hear the hum of excited voices coming from the cafeteria.

Gamma pulled it out. "When we feed it to the tiny man, he'll turn right back into himself."

"But . . . but Otto. He's got Skye in his locker," blubbered Barton.

Nancy pointed around the corner.

It was time for some pinkie power. Gamma and I powered up our boots. Sticking out our little fingers, we swooped over Otto's head.

Swatting him on the head, we shouted, *"MUCKA MUCKA!"*

"What . . . what's going on?" yelled Otto, looking up. "That's Barton. And Nancy. Flying above in the air . . . like Superman . . . wait a minute." He whipped around and stared at Nancy and Barton. "You're behind me. And above me. This is freaky . . . there's two of you . . . above and behind. Above and behind! But you . . . you two have antennae growing out of your heads!"

"That's because we're Barton and Nancy's alien clones from outer space," I explained. "From the planet Ungapotch. We landed a couple of weeks ago in the Dumpster. You'd remember this, Earthling, except we have sucked out your brain cells many times."

As Otto screamed we used our *mucka mucka* pinkie power to open up his locker. Barton grabbed Otto's backpack and pulled out the Cracker Jack box, and then he threw the backpack onto the floor.

Otto hid his face. "It's freaky . . . your pinkie. Aliens! Help! Infestation!"

As Otto raced away Barton and Nancy zoomed up to the room behind the stage in the cafeteria and closed the door. Gamma and I fired up our boots to hyperwarp speed to avoid detection and joined them.

Nancy held the box of Cracker Jack. "Skye?" she asked. "Are you okay? Skye?"

There was silence. Then a faint mumble. It sounded like a mad mumble.

As Nancy opened the top Skye flung pieces of Cracker Jack. One of them beaned me on the neck.

"Oh, Skye, I'm so, so sorry," said Barton. "We'll make it up to you. We promise. It's just that our alien clones from outer space got a little confused."

"Your what?" asked Skye. "Look, I don't know what's going on here, but I don't like it. Make me big. Get me out of this box of Cracker Jack!"

Nancy helped Skye out of the box and then placed him carefully on the floor.

Gamma presented the minuscule earthling with the antidote.

"Eat this, and everything will be okay," I said.

"That color was extracted from the Ungapotchian moon," said Gamma. "All of the moons of Ungapotch are pink."

"Hey," said Skye. "There's four of you."

"We're uh . . . quadruplets," said Nancy.

"I need a vacation," said Skye, shaking his head. "More rest." He stared at the antidote. It resembled the planet Ungapotch, if the planet had coconut frosting and pink sprinkles. "You expect me to take a bite out of that? You've got to be crazy. That's the size of a basketball."

"It's the only thing in the universe that's going to make you big again," I stated.

"Listen to him, Skye," pleaded Barton.

Skye sniffed and then held his nose. "It smells like seaweed. Like feet. I can't eat that. It's gross."

"Skye, you've got to," I said. "It's the only way!"

"Please, Skye," begged Nancy. "Pretty please with sugar on top. Do you want to be the size of a Tootsie Roll forever?"

Chapter 11

BARTON:
Don't Get Caught Short

Opening his mouth, Skye jumped up like he had springs in his shoes. Only, he fell backward. "I can't eat this thing," he said, moaning. "It's too hard."

I turned to Beta. "Can you do something? Make it softer?"

Beta nodded. "I will try to oxidize it with the *xactro* ray." He whipped out a shiny-looking tube that had little orange flashing lights. When he pointed the tube at the ball thingie, it started to soften. Little pieces of pink melted right off of it.

"The antidote has been oxidized," Gamma said.

Opening his mouth, Skye clamped his teeth onto the pink ball. "Now it's slimy."

Then someone knocked on the door. "Skye! It's Adam Bell from the *Pine Bluff Herald.* I'm here for the interview. You promised me at least one good quote."

"I remember," said Skye in his squeaky helium voice.

Another knock on the door. "Skye, open up," insisted Mr. Dumpsy. "The photographers want to take some photos."

My heart hammered. It was the principal!

"Can't come in," I yelled. "No!" I ran up against the door. Nancy joined me. "The door's locked," I said.

"Skye, I'm so sorry," said Mr. Dumpsy's voice. "We'll fix this in a jiffy."

Another bang on the door again. "It's Adam Bell, the reporter. Do you have anything to say?"

"Be thankful you're taller than a pencil!" said Skye in a little voice.

"Eat," I whispered, pointing to the antidote.

He took another bite.

Skye's left ear started to grow. It flapped around like an elephant's, and he tumbled over. Then his other ear got bigger. Finally, the rest of him started to grow too.

Soon Skye was three feet tall.

Nancy held out the pink ball of slime. "Eat more!"

Skye gulped down another bite.

"HELP IS ON ITS WAY!" screamed Principal Dumpsy. "The assembly is about to start in one minute. But don't worry, Skye. I've called for the custodian. He's going to bust open the door with a sledgehammer! We'll be right back."

Nancy and I looked at each other. This was not good. This was really, really bad.

When Skye grew to five feet, we felt a teeny bit better. But not much, because that's when I heard Otto's voice.

"Open this door!" he yelled. "I've got a dozen national reporters right here! If you open up right now, you will see what I'm talking about. It will be a world scoop. Skye Johnston is right behind this door and he's two inches tall. I saw him with my own eyes. He's with Barton and Nancy, and they have alien clones from outer space!"

"You've got to be kidding me," said a gruff man's voice.

"No, it's true!" screamed Sarge. "Those two

freaks flew over my head and stole the hair off *my* chin!"

"Hey, who knows?" said another voice. "I've heard crazier things. Skye, it's Frank Silvers from Channel Three. Are you in there? Are you two inches tall?"

"Yes!" yelled Skye.

"Quick, suck out his brain cells!" I yelled. In hyperwarp speed Beta took out his brain Slurpee straw and sucked out Skye's memory cells.

"Yes what?" asked the reporter from the *Pine Bluff Herald*.

"Yes, you're crazy, and no, I'm not two inches tall," said Skye.

Bang! Bang! Bang!

"Then, why won't you open up that door, if you have nothing to hide?" screamed Otto.

Skye kept on eating. His cheeks blew up like a chipmunk's.

His legs shot out. And then his head expanded like a balloon.

I clapped. "Way to go, Beta and Gamma. It's working."

But Skye kept on expanding. His legs must

have been ten feet tall. His head was about to shoot through the roof.

"He's, like, tree big!" Nancy screamed. "He's supposed to be only seven feet tall."

"HELP!" roared Skye.

"Feed him some more *blip-sprock*," said Gamma, taking a dish out of her backpack. "Eat some of this. Just a little amount."

Another bang on the door. "It's Principal Dumpsy. We've got a sledgehammer! So we're going to bust down the door. Ready? One . . . two . . ."

At that moment Nancy and I sprinted away from the door. "The lock is fixed," I said.

The door flew open. Mr. Dumpsy and the custodian, Mr. Reynolds, burst into the room. A gaggle of reporters was right behind them.

I closed my eyes. I couldn't look at Skye. And the clones were in the room with us. They'd be discovered. This was a nightmare!

But everyone seemed to be laughing and acting normal. What was going on? Peeking through my fingers, I stared at Skye.

He was his normal size again!

But where were the clones? I searched every-
where. When my eyes glanced up at two pairs of
antennae.

The clones were hiding in the rafters. I
breathed a huge sigh of relief.

"Hey, Skye," said Principal Dumpsy, slapping
Skye on the back. "Glad to see everything's okay.
These youngsters treating you all right?"

"Oh, yeah!" said Skye. "They're my buddies."

"Ready for the show?" asked Mr. Dumpsy.
"We've got the basketball net all set up onstage."

Skye nodded.

"But . . . but," babbled Otto. "They're alien
clones, and they shrank Skye!"

"And they stole my chin hairs!" exclaimed
Sarge.

Mr. Dumpsy shook his head. "Mrs. Denzer, you
need a vacation." He pulled out a pink slip and
waved it. "Otto, I've got a little present for you."

Then Mr. Dumpsy pulled open the curtain.
"The one, the only—Skye Johnston!" Skye
walked onto the stage. Mr. Dumpsy handed Skye
a giant, gold-sprayed cardboard key. "Here's the
key to our school!"

All of the kids went nuts, stomping their feet and clapping wildly.

Skye motioned for Nancy and me to walk over to his side. I couldn't believe it. Skye grinned. "These are my buddies, Barton and Nancy." He waved his arms. "Read books, kids. It'll open up your dreams! And eat only food cooked in low-saturated oil. Now, let's shoot baskets!"

Skye effortlessly pushed the ball into the air. It swished into the basket. Then he handed the ball over to Nancy. "Your turn."

Nancy pumped the ball into the basket. Everyone screamed, "Two points!"

Next Skye threw the ball to me. "Your turn, buddy."

Cameras flashed. A bunch of kids screamed my name. I felt like a superstar.

Dribbling past my sister, I went for a layup. The ball banged against the backboard. It bounced into the air, landing on Otto's head. A bunch of kids giggled.

"OW!" he screamed. "Loser! Fart Bart!"

But I didn't care.

I was standing next to Skye Johnston.

As more cameras flashed Skye signed my basketball card and the back of Nancy's shirt. It was a great day on an amazing planet.

I smiled and waved up at the clones. They were the best. I couldn't imagine life without them.

I kept on smiling. Until I saw something onstage. It looked like a mouse. Yes, it was a mouse. He was eating something. I squinted my eyes. It looked like *uta-goola*, the stuff that makes everything giant. IT WAS *UTA-GOOLA*!

Uh-oh. Time to call the clones . . . again. . . .

Don't miss any of the
out-of-this-world adventures of the

Two Heads Are Better Than One

Who Let the Dogs Out?

The Baby-Sitters Wore Diapers

Written by H. B. Homzie
Illustrated by Matt Phillips

From Aladdin Paperbacks
Published by Simon & Schuster